Text and illustrations Copyright © 1977 by Marc Brown
All Rights Reserved
Addison-Wesley Publishing Company, Inc.
Reading, Massachusetts 01867
Printed in the United States of America
ABCDEFGHIJK-CP-7987

Library of Congress Cataloging in Publication Data

Brown, Marc Tolon
 Marc Brown's Full house

 SUMMARY: Three stories relate the activities
of a monster family, a character named Frisbee
and his friends, and a perfect pet.
 [1. Monsters--Fiction. 2. Pets--Fiction.
3. Friendship--Fiction. 4. Short stories.
5. Picture books.] I. Title.
PZ7.B81618Mar   [E]   77-7962
ISBN 0-201-00341-4

MARC BROWN'S FULL HOUSE

♠ Addison-Wesley

THIS BOOK IS DEDICATED WITH LOVE TO MY FAMILY
♡ STEPHANIE, TOLON, AND TUCKER ♡

THE MONSTER FAMILY

PAPA

MAMA

Romeo
THE PERFECT PET

SPENCER

FRISBEE'S FRIENDS

FRISBEE ←

 GRANDMA
 GRANDPA
 SISTER
 BROTHER

 ISADORA
 CYNTHIA
 BASIL

HIS FRIENDS ⟶

Romeo

THE PERFECT PET

| CYNTHIA | ISADORA | BASIL |

I'll admit, I was fussy. I only ate sardines.

I liked to sharpen my claws.

I didn't get along with Cynthia, the canary.

And I preferred to spend my evenings out.

When they started criticizing the crowd I ran around with, I knew it was time to leave. One night I went out and never came home.

They didn't like Cynthia because she would only talk at night.

She would bite anyone who tried to clean her cage.

She liked a dirty cage.

They said she was a nasty bird.

Someone finally left her cage door open and she flew away.

They didn't like Basil because he'd splash water on the good table.

Then he'd hide in his castle for days.

He wouldn't eat his fish food.

And he started to swim funny.

One day Basil floated to the top of the bowl.

They didn't like Isadora because she had accidents on the rug.

She would make them sneeze.

She liked to sit on the living-room furniture.

And she had four puppies.

They took Isadora to a farm where she and her puppies would have more room to run.

The other day I was passing their house, and I looked in the window.
They had a new pet.
He doesn't eat expensive food.
He doesn't squawk at night.
He doesn't have accidents on the rug.
He doesn't make anyone sneeze.
He doesn't do anything.
They call him Romeo, the perfect pet.

Who is Marc Brown and where did this book come from?

Things I like:
Watching things grow, playing with my sons, eating green things, touching fuzzy things, screaming, crying, running, doing sit-ups, push-ups, chin-ups, being alone sometimes, traveling, eating ice cream, breakfast in bed, drawing, painting, watching the sunrise over the ocean, chickens, taking showers, listening to people, laughing, making new friends and making the best books I can.

About this book:
All of the characters are people I know who remind me of animals. All people remind me of animals and colors. I think people are funny and beautiful. To draw the pictures for this book I used watercolors, colored pencils, magic markers, gouache and a variety of black lines. I like this book very much. It has a good beat and it's easy to dance to. Out of a possible 100, I give it a 97.